For Odette, who loves
B. B.

For Miss Dove and Miss McLeod
K. M. D.

First published 2014 by Walker Books Ltd
87 Vauxhall Walk, London SE11 5HJ

This edition published 2015

2 4 6 8 10 9 7 5 3 1

Text © 2014 Bonny Becker
Illustrations © 2014 Kady MacDonald Denton

The right of Bonny Becker and Kady MacDonald Denton to be identified as
author and illustrator respectively of this work has been asserted by them
in accordance with the Copyright, Designs and Patents Act 1988

This book has been typeset in New Baskerville

Printed in China

British Library Cataloguing in Publication Data:
a catalogue record for this book is available from the British Library

ISBN 978-1-4063-6093-6

www.walker.co.uk

A Library Book for Bear

Bonny Becker

illustrated by
Kady MacDonald Denton

WALKER BOOKS
AND SUBSIDIARIES
LONDON • BOSTON • SYDNEY • AUCKLAND

Bear had never been to the library.
He had seven very nice books at home:
three about kings and queens, three about honey-bees
and one about pickles.
Bear was quite sure he had
all the books he would ever need.

One morning, Bear heard a *tap, tap, tapping* on his door.

When he opened the door, there was Mouse, small and grey and bright-eyed.

"We're off!" exclaimed Mouse with a happy wag of his whiskers.

Bear frowned. He had agreed to go with Mouse to the library, but now he was quite sure it was a dreadful mistake.

"Completely unnecessary," Bear announced. "I have all the books I need right here."

"Oh, there are many delightful books in the library," Mouse assured him.

"Hmmph!" Bear grumbled – but he *had* promised.

So he buckled up his red roller skates and stepped outside, grabbing a basket for the books.

Bear skated and Mouse rode in the basket to the library, the wind rippling nicely through their fur.

But when they got to the library, Bear thought it looked much too big.

"There are far too many books in there," he protested. "Most excessive!"

"Oh, no. It's quite exciting," Mouse said, leading Bear through the tall doors.

In the library were more books than Bear had ever thought there could be.
He quickly found a tucked-away corner. But even here, there were lots and
lots of books.

"Hmmph! Terribly extravagant!" Bear's voice was a little loud.

"I shall find you the perfect one," Mouse said quietly in his library voice.

"One about pickles," commanded Bear. After all, he had only one of those.

But Mouse had whisked away.

Mouse came back with a thick green book. Bear opened it.

"Rocket ships! Ridiculous!" Bear's voice was getting louder. "A good
book about pickles is all I require!"

"Remember – quiet in the library," murmured Mouse as he scurried off.

He soon returned with a tall yellow book.

"I am not interested in wooden canoes!"

Bear's voice was even louder.

"Quiet voices in the library," Mouse reminded him.

"My voice is always quiet," Bear shouted.
"I will find my own book. I can assure
you that pickles are quite interesting!"

Mouse didn't look so sure. But Bear quickly spotted a blue book with a pickle on the spine, and Mouse sprang up to the shelf to get it for him.

Inside were pictures of pickles. The pickles had little fairy wings.

They were dancing with petunias.

"NO DANCING PICKLES!" Bear roared.

"SHHHHHHHH!" said a voice.

Bear peeked round a bookshelf.

There sat a librarian with a cluster of youngsters gathered around her.
The librarian smiled, but a mother squirrel squished an angry finger
against her lips, and an old raccoon said sternly, "Quiet in the library."

Bear turned back with a huffy sniff. "I know when

I'm not wanted," he told Mouse. "I want to go home."

"Surely, at least one book—" Mouse began.

But Bear cut him off: "I have all the books I need."

He looked quite certain.

"Then we're off," said Mouse, but his whiskers didn't wag this time.

Bear stood stock-still. He was listening carefully to a voice on the other side of the bookshelf.

"So the Very Brave Bear began to inch his way towards the treasure chest…"
the voice was saying.

"I'm ready—" began Mouse.

"SHHHHHHHHH!" exclaimed Bear.

"It's just getting to the good part!"

"But you said—"

"QUIET VOICES IN THE LIBRARY!"

Bear bellowed.

This time the librarian got up and looked round the bookshelf at Bear.

Bear stood very still and quiet, as if he had been still and quiet all along.

"Would you like to join story time?" the librarian asked.

Bear glanced at Mouse.

"We'd love to have you," said the librarian.

Bear and Mouse scooted round the shelf and found two empty chairs.

The librarian began to read again.

"Bear lifted the lid of the treasure chest, and inside…"

The librarian paused. Mouse and Bear strained forwards.

"*Inside,*" she said, "*was a mound of pickle slices. And each shining slice was made of diamonds and gold! And everyone shouted, 'Hooray for the Very Brave Bear!'*"

And then she said, "*The end.*"

Bear stared dreamily into space for a moment. Then he looked over at Mouse and announced, "As I said, pickles are most interesting."

"Indeed," said Mouse.

Later, Mouse rode in the basket with seven new books. There were two about wooden canoes, two about rocket ships, two about teapots …

and one called *The Very Brave Bear and the Treasure of Pickle Island,*

which Bear read to Mouse that very same day.